Bamboo & Friends
The Moon

by Felicia Law
illustrated by Nicola Evans

Editor: Jacqueline A. Wolfe
Page Production: Tracy Davies
Creative Director: Keith Griffin
Editorial Director: Carol Jones
Managing Editor: Catherine Neitge

First American edition published in 2006 by
Picture Window Books
5115 Excelsior Boulevard
Suite 232
Minneapolis, MN 55416
877-845-8392
www.picturewindowbooks.com

Printed in the United States of America.

Library of Congress Cataloging-in-Publication Data
Law, Felicia.
The moon / by Felicia Law ; illustrated by Nicola Evans.— 1st
American ed.
p. cm. — (Bamboo & friends)
Summary: Three friends, settling down to sleep in their magical
forest home, share what they know about the moon.
ISBN 1-4048-1282-2 (hardcover)
[1. Moon—Fiction. 2. Rain forest animals—Fiction.] I. Evans,
Nicola, ill. II. Title. III. Series.
PZ7.L41835Mo 2005
[E]—dc22   2005007186

Bamboo, Velvet, and Beak sit on their log in the middle of the magical forest, just as they always do.

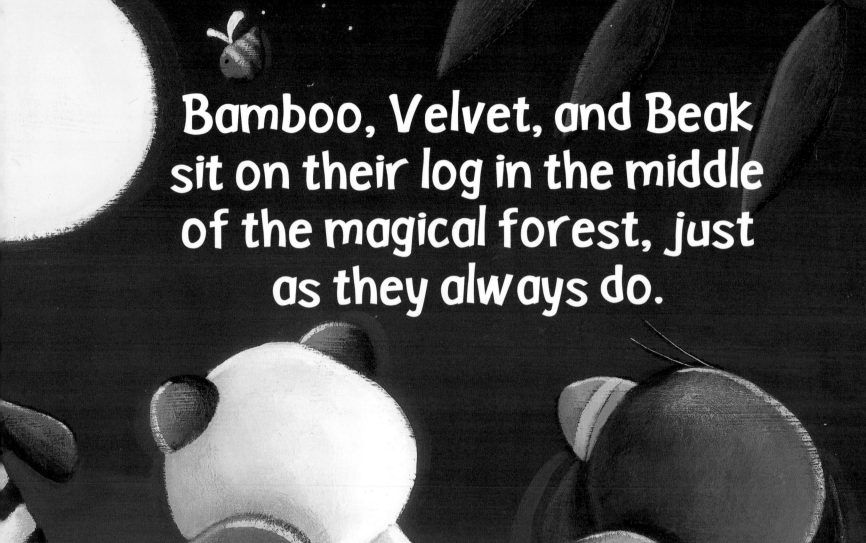

They gaze at the night sky.
"That light is on again,"
says Bamboo.

"Which light?" Beak asks.

"That light in the sky," answers Bamboo.

"It's called the moon," says Beak.

6

The moon's surface has hilly areas from craters and some smooth plains, too.

"And it's not a light. It's a cold lump of rock," says Velvet.

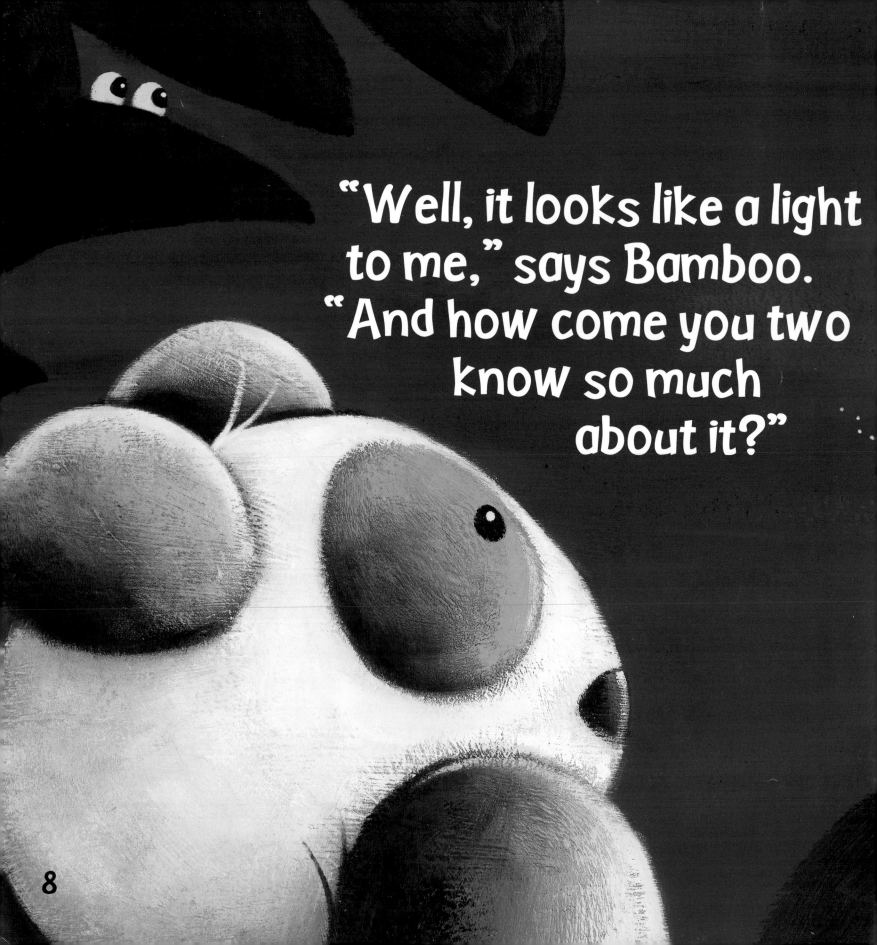

"Well, it looks like a light to me," says Bamboo. "And how come you two know so much about it?"

8

9

The first people landed on the moon in 1969.

10

"Some people went up there,"
says Velvet.
"They traveled through
space in a rocket.
It was a great adventure."

"A rocket is a space machine," says Beak.

12

"I know
what a rocket is,"
says Bamboo.

13

So what happened when they got there?" asks Bamboo.

Neil Armstrong was the first person to step on the moon.

14

"They looked around and came home again," says Velvet.

15

16

"Doesn't sound like much of an adventure to me," says Bamboo.

"Why would you go all that way in a rocket just to see a cold lump of rock?" asks Bamboo.

18

Scientists study the moon to help answer many different questions about the moon and space.

19

"Unless, of course, the light went out! Then they would need to replace the bulb," adds Bamboo sleepily.

20

"Because it sure is nice to have a night light," Bamboo says.

23

Fun Facts

- Michael Collins piloted the Apollo 1,160 miles (1,856 kilometers) from the moon's surface. Neil Armstrong and Buzz Aldin traveled in only the fourth lunar module that had ever been flown. There were no seats, so they were held in place by elastic cords.

- Armstrong and Aldrin spent two hours and 31 minutes walking on the moon's surface. During this time, they were able to prepare a solar wind collector, ready a laser reflector for action, raise an American flag, gather 47 pounds (7.7 kilograms) of samples, and take about 100 color photos.

- There were 12 astronauts who explored the surface of the moon from 1969 to 1972.

- The moon is the second brightest object in Earth's sky, next to the sun.
- As the moon circles Earth, the shape of the moon appears to change. This is because different parts of the illuminated moon are facing us.

- The moon's shape is smallest, or what we call the new moon, when the moon is between the sun and Earth.

- When the moon looks like a big circle in the sky, it is called a full moon.

- The moon doesn't produce its own light; it looks bright because it reflects light from the sun. Think of the sun as the light bulb and the moon as a mirror reflecting light from the light bulb.

On the Web

FactHound offers a safe, fun way to find Internet sites related to this book. All of the sites on FactHound have been researched by our staff.

Here's how:

1. Visit www.facthound.com

2. Type in this special code for age-appropriate sites: 1404812822

3. Click on the FETCH IT button.

Your trusty FactHound will fetch the best sites for you!

Look for all of the books about Bamboo & Friends: